AR Quiz No# 68288 EN
BL# 2.7
AR Pts.# 0.5

Lionel's Birthday

Lionel's Birthday

by Stephen Krensky
pictures by Susanna Natti

DIAL BOOKS FOR YOUNG READERS
New York

For Ellen and Emily Cohen
S.K.

To Grace and David Murray
S.N.

Published by Dial Books for Young Readers
A division of Penguin Young Readers Group
345 Hudson Street
New York, New York 10014
Text copyright © 2003 by Stephen Krensky
Pictures copyright © 2003 by Susanna Natti
Manufactured in China on acid-free paper
The Dial Easy-to-Read logo is a registered trademark of
Dial Books for Young Readers, a division of Penguin Group (USA) Inc.
® TM 1,162,718.
1 3 5 7 9 10 8 6 4 2

Library of Congress Cataloging-in-Publication Data
Krensky, Stephen.
Lionel's birthday / by Stephen Krensky ; pictures by Susanna Natti.
p.   cm.
Summary: Lionel counts down the days to his birthday party by making a
time capsule and by letting his sister know what he wants for a present.
ISBN 0-8037-2752-6
[1. Birthdays—Fiction. 2. Brothers and sisters—Fiction.]
I. Natti, Susanna, ill. II. Title.
PZ7.K883 Lmf 2003   [E]—dc21   2001008501

The full-color artwork was prepared using pencil,
colored pencils, and watercolor washes.

Reading Level 2.2

CONTENTS

THE PRESENT

Lionel was lying on the living room floor

looking under the couch.

"Not here," he said to himself.

Then he checked in the back

of the hall closet.

"Not here either."

Lionel kept looking—

down in the basement,

up in the attic,

even in the doghouse.

Finally, he went to Louise's room.

"Okay, Louise," said Lionel.

"I give up."

"About what?" asked Louise.

Lionel sighed.

"I've looked everywhere.

Well, except for the roof,

or up the chimney,

or in the tree out back, or—"

"*Lionel!*" Louise interrupted.

"What *are* you talking about?"

"My birthday present," said Lionel.

"The one from you.

I can't find it."

"Of course you can't find it," said Louise.

"What do you mean, *of course*?"

said Lionel.

"I'm very good at finding things."

"That may be," said Louise.

"But you can't find your birthday present

because I haven't gotten it yet."

Lionel was shocked. "You haven't?"

Louise shook her head.

"But Louise, there are only six days left

till my birthday."

"So?"

"So that's a lot of pressure,"

Lionel explained.

"Because I know you want to get me

just the right thing."

"I do?" Louise asked.

Lionel nodded. "That's why I'm willing

to help you out with a little hint,

to point you in the right direction."

"Okay," said Louise.

"Go ahead and hint."

"I want a jet pack," said Lionel.

"Some hint!" said Louise.

"What would you do with a jet pack?"

"Fly around the neighborhood," said Lionel.

"On weekends I might go farther—
maybe the North Pole or Mars."

Louise thought a moment.

"Sorry," she said,

"but if I gave you a jet pack,

it wouldn't be a surprise."

"Oh," said Lionel.

He hadn't thought of that.

Then he frowned.

"Wait a minute," he said.

"You shouldn't have told me

about the surprise being a surprise."

"Why not?" Louise asked.

"Because," said Lionel,

"it can't be a surprise

if I already *know* about it.

You'll have to think of something else."

"Like what?" Louise asked.

Lionel smiled.

"Like a jet pack," he said.

BURYING THE PAST

"Four days to go,"

Lionel said to his dog.

He was standing in his yard

leaning on a shovel.

"Hi, Lionel," said his friend Jeffrey,

coming around the corner.

"What are you doing?"

"I'm digging a hole,"

said Lionel.

Jeffrey took a closer look.

"It's very nice," he said.

"But what's it for?"

"My time capsule," Lionel explained.

"I'm going to put different things

from my life in it."

"Wow!" said Jeffrey.

"What made you think of doing that?"

Lionel patted the edge of the hole.

"I asked my father

what he remembered about his birthday

when he was my age.

He said it was all kind of fuzzy

because it happened so long ago."

Jeffrey nodded.

"My father says stuff like that too."

"But I won't forget," said Lionel.

"Years from now

I'll just dig up my time capsule,

and everything in it

will help me remember."

"So what are you putting inside?"

asked Jeffrey.

"My old baseball glove," said Lionel.

"A glow-in-the-dark circus button.

And my story about Spaceship Bob

and the Spinach Monsters."

Suddenly, Jeffrey gasped.

"What if you forget where the hole is?"

Lionel stopped to think.

"I'll make a map," he said.

"To mark the spot."

"But what if you lose the map?"
asked Jeffrey.

"Remember last year,

when we lost Ellen's gerbil

for all of recess?

Or the time we couldn't find that key

for the pirate's treasure chest?"

"The one we had actually put *in* the chest

to keep it safe?" said Lionel.

Jeffrey nodded.

Lionel saw his point.

"Maybe I should bury the map

in its own hole," he said.

"Perfect," said Jeffrey.

"That way you'll always know where it is."

Lionel smiled

and started digging a second hole.

He had been wondering why more people

didn't bury time capsules.

But now he understood.

Holding on to your memories

was definitely hard work.

He just hoped they were worth it.

MIRROR, MIRROR

Lionel's birthday was getting very close.

"Only one more day to go," he said,

staring at himself in the bathroom mirror.

Lionel turned his face to the left.

Then he turned his face to the right.

He was going to be older

in one more day.

But he didn't look older—not yet.

Lionel scrunched his face

and picked up his mother's eyebrow pencil.

Then he drew in a line

wherever he saw a crease.

"Hmmmm," said Lionel.

Now he looked like a father

with a hard job

who didn't get much sleep.

"Lionel, what are you doing?"

asked Mother, passing by.

"I'm trying to see what I'll look like

in the future," he told her.

"Okay," said Mother.

"But no beards or mustaches."

Lionel picked up some powder
and sprinkled it on his hair.
Now he was a grandfather
who liked taking walks in the park.
"Hey there, Lionel," said Father.
"What's up?"
"I'm looking into the future,"
said Lionel.

"All right," said Father.

"But make sure you clean up the future

when you're done."

Lionel nodded.

He patted some more powder

on his eyebrows

and put on his mother's reading glasses.

"Lionel, just *what* are you doing?"

asked Louise.

Lionel turned around.

"What do you *think* I'm doing?"

"I *think* you're making a mess," she said.

"No, no," he assured her.

"This is all very scientific.

I'm trying to see into the future.

Don't you think I'll look like this someday?"

Louise looked him over.

"Yes," she said. "I do."

"Really?" cried Lionel.

"Definitely," said Louise.

"And not just any time in the future either.

One very specific time."

Lionel was very excited.

He hadn't realized that Louise knew

so much about these things.

"What time will that be?" he asked.

Louise gave him a big smile.

"On Halloween," she said.

"You'll be just perfect."

Then she darted out of sight.

THE WISH

"Wake up, Lionel!" said Louise.

"Happy birthday!"

said Mother and Father.

Lionel opened his eyes.

His whole family was standing

around his bed.

His birthday was finally here!

At breakfast Lionel had toast

with jam and jelly and honey on it.

"Looks kind of gooey," said Louise.

Lionel smiled.

"The Birthday Boy can eat

whatever he wants," he said.

Then he began taking deep breaths.

"What are you doing?" asked Louise.

"Practicing for my party," said Lionel.

Later, everyone started to get ready.

Father baked a cake.

Mother and Louise put up the decorations.

Lionel went outside

and took more deep breaths.

Every year Lionel made a wish

before he blew out his candles.

But so far none of his wishes

had ever come true.

Lionel had always wondered why.

Now he knew it was because

he had never blown out

all the candles with one breath.

"Haaaaaahhh . . . paahhhhhhhh!
Haaaaahhh . . . paahhhhhhhh!"

"Why are you huffing and puffing?"

asked Mother.

"Are you planning to visit

the Three Little Pigs?"

Lionel shook his head.

"I'm still getting ready," he said.

"And there's not much time left."

At two o'clock, the party began.

Lionel and his friends

threw water balloons at a Slime Monster

and blasted cork rockets into space.

Then Lionel's father brought out the cake.

His mother lit the candles,

and everyone sang "Happy Birthday."

Lionel took a breath—

and then turned his head to let it out.

"Not big enough," he explained.

On his second try,

he sucked in air like a giant vacuum cleaner.

Then he blew.

"Whooooooosh!"

The candles fluttered for just a moment . . .

and then every single one of them went out.

"Hooray for Lionel!" his friends shouted.

"Way to go!"

"I'm glad the cake didn't blow over."

As his father cut the cake,

Louise tapped Lionel on the shoulder.

"So what was your wish?" she whispered.

"I can't tell you, Louise," he said.

"But maybe you can guess?"

Then he looked at his presents

and smiled, knowing that this year

his wish had come true.